Willy's Diary

The first months
of a foundling kitten

Narrated and photographed by
Thomas Preller

ISBN:
First unabbreviated English edition
© January 2016, Thomas Preller
This work is protected by copyright.
All rights, including excerpts exploitation rights are reserved.
Envelope concept: Thomas Preller
Envelope photos: Thomas Preller
English translation: Thomas Preller
All Photos and Illustrations © Thomas Preller
Production: BoD – Books on Demand, Norderstedt, Germany
The German National Library lists this publication in the
German National Library;
detailed bibliographic data are available in the Internet:
www.dnb.de.

A word from Willy at the beginning:
*"Please excuse my bad English, I'm just
a tiny cat and have to learn a lot".*

🐾 First Day: Darkness

I don't know how I came here. I just know that I felt a kick and fell on this lonely dirt road. I feel all alone. My mum and siblings are nowhere nearby. I can't see anything, I can only hear. Suddenly, I hear footsteps coming towards me and I'm really scared.

Maybe I should go in the direction where the footsteps come from?
Well, it can't be worse than it already is.
I feel so miserable, weak, thirsty, hungry and tired and anyway, I do want to know what to expect here.

I hear a voice saying:

"Hey, this little one looks just like the killer whale from the movie! He is so courageous, walking towards me like that. If it is a boy, I think the name Willy will suit him well."

A short time later I hear the same voice:

"No wonder that it comes to me as the eyes are totally stuck together and can't see anything at all. Say, where did you come from? Where are your mum and siblings?"

Well, you fast learner, now you seem to have realised that I cannot see.

I can feel and smell the scent of another strange cat next to me and the voice says: *"Hey, Mister Schiefkopf, is that one of your kids?"* But as quick as it came, the scent disappears again.

Suddenly, two warm hands touch me and lift me up.

"We should bring the little one to the farmer. He has an eye ointment on the shelf for emergencies that he received from the vet. The kitten is so dirty; look at the filthy coat."

Somehow I feel that the hands that surround me, want to do me no harm. So I keep quiet and wait for what comes next.

I am carried a short distance. Here it smells like many other animals that I do not know. One of these animals makes a noise that sounds like *'moo'*.

A short time later another friendly voice says,
"Where did you get it? I don't know this one."
Then I get a little slippery stuff rubbed above my nose. The voice of whoever it is, carries me and then says:

"Now you will get your eyes treated by the farmer. We will then take you back to the place where we found you. Maybe your Mummy is waiting for you. I've seen a cat there that looks so similar to you."

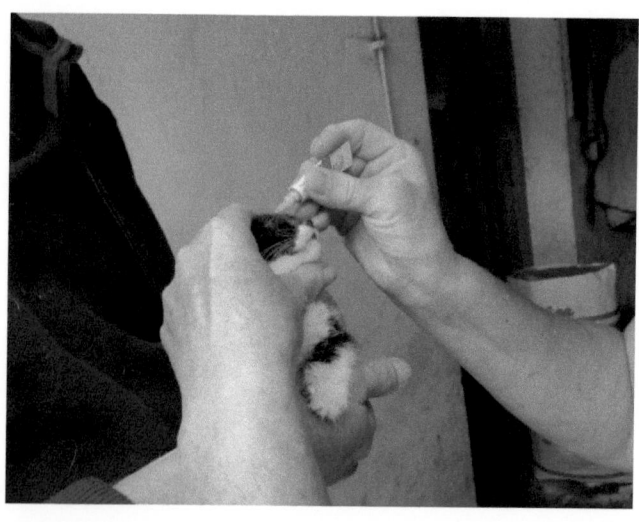

Again someone takes me a few steps further and places me on the ground. I hear two people discussing what they should do with me.

"We'll leave it here for the time being. It may well be that the mother cat finds him. Tomorrow we'll see if the little one is still there."

I feel that a little bowl is pushed towards me and someone gently pushes my mouth into it.

"Allright, fresh cow's milk for you. As weak as you are, you must be so hungry. This is quite a special treat and tastes really good!"
I don't feel like anything because I'm so tired and can barely move. I am gently stroked goodbye.

I don't know where I am. I don't know what was and what will be. The voices are now quite distant and I'm alone again. No siblings and no Mummy. I could just meow.

However, I am so weak that I can hardly stand on my feet again and I'm also so scared. The only things I hear are the loud noises of many iron animals that pass by quickly in the distance. People say they are called cars. It's feeling chilly around me. It's dark and I fall asleep.

Am I going to die now?

🖋 The start of a new life

"Look, it is still in the same place in the blazing midday sun! Is it still alive? It does not move."

The two voices that I heard yesterday begin to discuss what to do with me.

With my last strength, I lift my head, as they say, *"Look, it's still alive! Come on, let's take it to the vet now, otherwise it will not survive the day."*

I am gently lifted from the hard ground on which I slept and am smoothly stroked. This feels so good.

"Well, now we are looking for something with which to transport you in because there is no real cat basket available. A cardboard box will do for the moment until we get home."

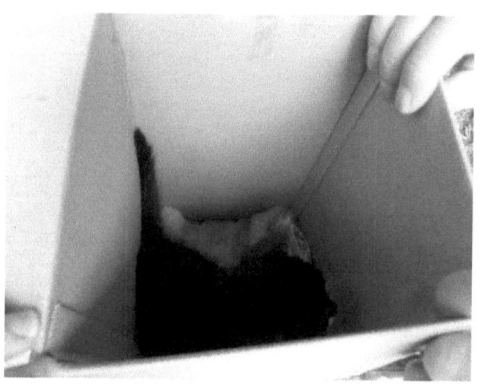

I am placed in the box and feel the lid close over me.

After a few steps in this comical narrow box, I'm dreadfully shaken. The people call it cycling and it is supposed to be healthy, but I don't like it. Although I'm protesting with my last strength, it's useless and the shaking continues.

Fortunately, the journey does not take long and I am transferred from the box in which I can hardly turn around, into a comfortable wicker with cushions. Oh, that's so soft. It feels really nice. There's plenty of space for me and air to breathe. It's so much more comfortable.

However, I really don't know what comes next and would love to be spared of it. Veterinary! In my case, a female vet, but I guess that does not make any difference at all.

So now I am also curious. Somehow this is all very funny. There are strange voices everywhere and strange scents of many different animals; yet also a smell of unbelievable cleanliness.

"What do we have here? This kitten's condition looks very bad! It was probably exposed on the farm. I've already seen a few cases of animal injustice in the past. The cats from the farm never look like this. So let's see what kind of cat you are."

I'm turned on my back, although I do not like this position and my hind legs are forced apart. What the heck are they doing with me?

"Ah, here we have a little boy in front of us. I guess he is about four weeks old. It doesn't look like he has eyes.

Well, on the left I see something at the back like an eye and at the right, nothing at all. At the moment everything is full of pus and I see almost only raw flesh. We'll have to wait for now and at worst he could remain blind. Now he'll get his first dose of antibiotics. Because he is completely dehydrated, also some water under the skin, even if it hurts terribly. There are no parasites in the fur, but he will definitely still be dewormed. In two days we'll meet again, then he will get the next antibiotic injection."

The vet uses her two fingers to touch my coat on the back, pulls it up and it just stays that way. This does not seem to be normal and it hurts me.

Maybe this is the reason why I'm so incredibly thirsty all the time.

Do I have to like veterinarians?

I have not given her permission to push a cold metallic thing in my butt for an alleged body temperature measurement; after all, we are not with *'Shades of grey'* or whatever it's called.

But now I'm still stuck on my back and I have hellish pain. Ouch! That hurts terribly! I don't want any needles in my back. Stop it immediately!

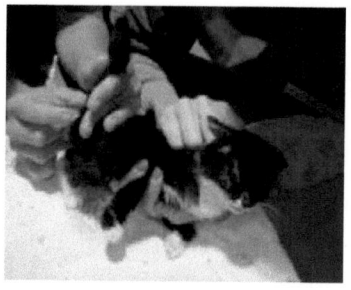

No, any amount of good persuasion won't help so I have to scream like hell because of the pain I feel.

Into the bargain the vet says, *"The belly feels very hard so I'm going to give him an enema just in case there also problems here."*

Enema? What's this? Once again I get something cold pushed into my butt and it gurgles quite terribly within me. Although I try to defend myself, there are just too many hands holding me still.

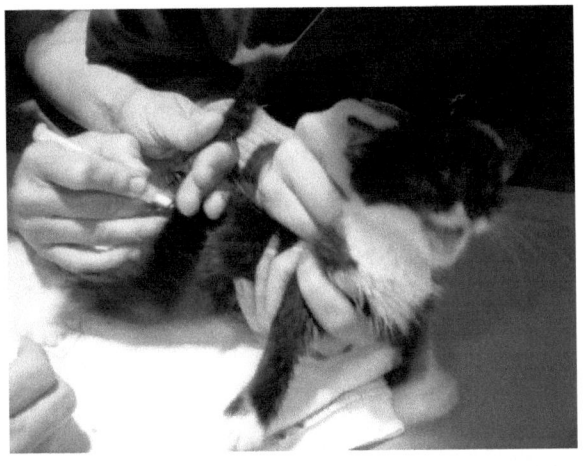

After two or three pricks into my back I hear, *"With a bottle of milk replacer every three hours and eye drops twice daily, perhaps this little one will get better soon. We can only hope that he survives at all. At the moment he is just hanging on because of his parched body. See you tomorrow. Hopefully you'll be back."*

My health status seems quite bad when I hear the words of the vet. But bottles of milk sound good. About the eye drops, I'm not quite so sure.

As exhausted and weak as I am, my will to live is still unbroken.

"So you're a boy," says the voice, which has brought me here.
"Then we will probably call you Willy, after the famous Orca from the movie. It does suit you well."

How the heck does this guy know what suits me and if I like this name at all? Well, it could have been much worse. I am really happy that they didn't choose the name Samson or Puppet. The other bright voice that I already heard yesterday says, *"You've really fallen from the sky"* and I don't know at all what she means.

I'm placed back into the basket. Where are they carrying me to now? *"First you'll come with us, because we will introduce you to Aunt Molly, Aunt Salsa and Aunt Lola."*

Aunts? Which aunts? I don't know that I have relatives. It's a bit fishy to me but right now I'm too tired to think about it and besides, I want to forget all the stress from being at the vet.

Even before we arrive at our destination, the effects are seen from this enema. This is really embarrassing for me now but by the way they carry me around in the basket, I can't help it. I just don't have any more power to detain it. Interestingly however, the voices seem glad about my mishap.

Curling up to sleep will now be best for me. At this new place, there are many new smells and sounds. Actually, since my birth, I'm very curious and I would like to know what the place smells and looks like as well as get to know the two voices that I hear all the time. It is all completely different than I've experienced before in my short life.

I can't even tell that I am closing my eyes because I do not know if I have any at all. Then I begin to dream of what it was like when my siblings and I used to snuggle and nuzzle together in the nest with our Mum, while she purred and licked our fur clean with her warm and rough tongue.

Superb, what a wonderful dream!

🐾 The feeding bowl pack

The next morning, I still can't see anything yet, but I can smell excellently. Although I am still very tired, I smell other cats!
I hear hissing, purring and growling noises.

"Howdy Willy, I am Molly."

"I was born here in this house and have lived here nine years since then. My dad moved out a few years ago and shortly thereafter my mum died. I didn't even know about it.

Because of my age I am the quietest cat in this house but am mostly outside where I can catch a lot of mice.

If you can keep a secret, I'll tell you that I have a mate whom you'll meet later.

You smell terrible, just as if you'd come from the vet.
Whenever I have to go there, I start to tremble, hackle and my fur begins to falls out.

Some good advice from me: I need a long time to warm up to someone, regardless of whether they are cats or humans, so behave yourself decently in my presence."

Molly actually sounds quite nice and her voice makes a pretty level-headed impression. She seems to be quite reasonable and I don't think I need to be afraid of her, because she purrs the whole time.

"Good day to you, I'm Salsa and I'm from France, more precisely from the beautiful French Basque country. For half a year now I live here with my daughter Lola.

My Maman left France for a new love and moved more than two thousand miles to this place, with us in her small car. I'm tricolored, wear fashionable harem pants and I'm also of course the fairest in all the whole country."

"Just trust me: This Karl, or how this fashion designer is named, would have much joy with my bitching and if someone doesn't like me, I will make a sound like the start of a 'Formula 1' race. Because I am so beautiful, you can pay homage to me every day."

I have the vague feeling that there is actually a real bitch in front of me because of the tone in her voice with her subliminal, snide accent. This Aunt Salsa seems to be a real diva.

But maybe she's really very cute, even if she does grumble and hiss.

"What is dis littöl black devil doing eere? I am Lola, the daugtöör of Salsa and ave problööms with dis languagöö. I am good at growliing, hissiing and eatiing the whole day and am always ungrii. The bowls in dis ouse are all mine."

(Authors translation: Lola claims all the bowls in the house; is totally greedy, on a diet and in desperation, starts to catch all the mice and rats in the area. Besides, she will probably never get rid of her French accent.)

From what I can hear, she can growl and hiss really well, but I'm not really that scared of her.

I think it sounds rather like a theatrical thunder so she does not have to share the food with the other cats, because she is so incredibly greedy. Often it's a kind of 'eating out of frustration', just like in the case with some people when they are totally dissatisfied with everything.

When she sleeps in her basket, a front paw and a hind paw usually hang over the basket edge. She also sleeps quite a lot and is negotiating to star in a movie called *'Run Lola Run'*.

Gosh, three aunts? Well, that'll be fun, but certainly it's better than sitting on a lonely dirty road with no food, no roof over my head and really with nothing at all. These scents are all so new and strange but at the moment I'm too exhausted to think about anything. I do feel quite well at this place.

Then something soft is gently pushed into my mouth now, but wait, that's warm and tastes heavenly!

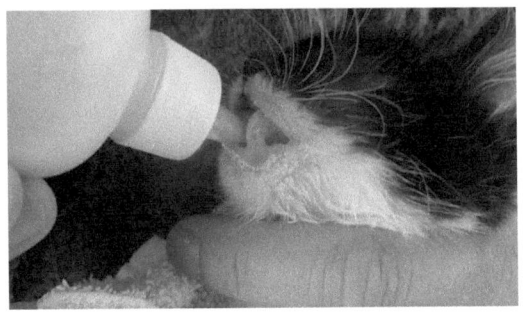

This tastes almost like the milk from Mummy, which I can hardly remember much anymore. Oh, that's so good. Then I even get a pleasant tummy massage. Frankly, it seems to me that I ended up in a luxurious spa hotel.

"Drink it, little Willy," says the voice that holds me and pushes this plastic teat back into my mouth. Phew, I can't drink anymore, but somehow a full belly feels really great. Carefully, I'm lifted and placed onto something cold.

"Your weight is now 340 Grams. Let's see if you get more meat on your ribs as quickly as possible."

The hands put me back into the transport cage. I am placed onto a warm cosy towel which feels really wonderful. It is quiet; there are no noises that can scare me.

Now as I go to sleep, I am considering whether I should write a personal diary because I have a vague feeling that here where I landed, a lot will happen.

🐾 Staff decisions

After spending some of the night thinking, I make the decision to move here, even if no one else has noticed yet. The people who have welcomed me, and currently I only know their voices, seem to be my future staff. I'll call them Daddy and Mommy from now on.

Yes I know, dogs usually do this, but it just sounds stupid to call them *'Can Openers'*, because I may not only get canned food. Perhaps I will also get other goodies or I may even catch mice outside. Somehow, you have to stand out from the crowd if you want to be a special someone nowadays. My staff's education hasn't begun early enough, so I'll start now with this. As a gentle introduction, I will immediately determine if my own dedicated staff will adapt to my daily schedule.

Today I heard Daddy say, *"Well Mommy, I placed a few pictures of Willy onto the Internet. Maybe someone from the 'Cats Group' will adopt him. After all, we already have three cats at home, and a fourth one? Well, I do not know if it's good ..."*

Gosh, they want to get rid of me and kick me out of the house? I sincerely believe that Daddy is nuts. I don't want to go away. At least I have a place to sleep here and plenty of food. He should sleep over it and then we'll see. I am sure I can manage this and Mommy is already on my side. I can tell by how she talks about me.

As soon as I fall asleep, I feel that my transport basket is lifted and after a short time, I'm back on the vet's treatment table.

"So, how's the little one today?"

Again I get the next painful twinge in my back.

"The antibiotics syringe is sorely needed, but you can already see the first signs of progress in the eye sockets. Maybe he is lucky that at some point, he will at least see something with one eye. We have to wait at least a week. The fur definitely looks better than the first time."

Interestingly, when one is held by so many hands, movement is quite limited. This suits me less and less and I'm slowly starting to complain about it.

Luckily the visit today doesn't take as long as two days ago. A short time later I am put back into the basket and am going to my new home.

🐾 Lights on!

Meanwhile, a few days have passed and I spend much time drinking and sleeping. That's actually quite pleasant, but what really bothers me is the fact that I'm wrapped twice a day up to my head in a towel and my new Daddy and Mommy put these ridiculous wet drops onto the spots where my eyes should be. It burns terribly and I cannot defend myself!

So now I'll show them how it feels by digging my claws and teeth into their skin. They don't have to mean. I don't have to put up with this at my young age. But somehow Daddy is always more powerful than me. The burning in my eyes subsides a short time later. I have definitely decided to protest regularly and maybe it will help in the long run.

From now on, towels are my future enemies and must be killed!

But what is that? Suddenly I can see light and darkness! Something moves in front of me! Well, that's great, finally I am no longer only limited to hearing and smelling. Now I can already see a bit of what's going on around me. While it still all looks very murky and I can only see outlines, it must have something to do with these eye drops.

My staff has now invented something else which is called eye ointment. Well, it's still not even better and this stuff burns just like the drops. I just do not understand why they do this to me. However, I suppose they do already know what's best for me.

Staff can really be annoying, but today I heard that Mommy and Daddy have decided to keep me permanently. Phew, what a big sigh of relief! I am reminded that they are actually quite nice, even if Daddy is sometimes nuts and talks nonsense.

My plan worked: I'll manage the rules in this house and everything that is not nailed down will be my possession. Regarding the aunts, it's a question of time. I will handle them and for sure, eventually they will only dance to my tune.

With every day, that I get this weird eye ointment administered and with my vigorous cries and resistance in the form of scratching and biting, I slowly see more outlines of light and dark.

I'm afraid of these great vertical pounding gizmos that people call 'feet and legs'. I should better run away and find a place to hide.

Left from the kitchen is a small hole which I just barely fit through and hide. My aunts can't catch me there; even my staff can't. If these legs should get too close to me, in any case I'll bite them as much as I can. Surely I won't do that much harm.

🐾 Half digested is well pooped

Meanwhile, I not only get my flask of delicious milk, but also something that's called meat. Wow, it tastes so good; it's to die for.

"Willy, you shall not get into the food with your feet! This is not respectable for a well mannered cat."
I once again hear a familiar voice, but I always let them talk while I do my own thing.

Throughout the day they say, *"Don't do this and don't do that,"* which I can't stand any longer. That's why I did a cunning thing and blamed the mites in my ears so I just can't listen to what the staff says. One must be sly.

Daddy and Mommy should be thankful, because after all, I'm so nice and do my 'business' in a sand-filled container which the people call a 'litter box' and it is said to have been sung about by a comedian. That's funny, because otherwise it is always called the quiet place. Scratching around in it with my paws makes a lot of noise and it is so much fun.

It always causes me to smile when I hear Daddy:
"Yeah Willy, you produce such beautiful sand dunes on the kitchen floor and your private bathroom attendant immediately cleans up this mess."

So Daddy is here and is really quite understanding. Every day I will probably make a few dunes on the kitchen floor, so he realises that he is a good servant. Every time while sweeping, he speaks about a desert planet. However, I do not know what it means when he says that he has not found any *'spice'* in the sand, but rather something completely different like sandworms.

I can't quite yet see the litter tray properly, but I usually go by the smell because it smells so fresh before I use it.

I would like to play with Aunt Molly, but

 somehow, she is not interested in me when she is at home. Maybe it is because she was born an only kitten. She recently told me that she had no siblings.

Aunt Salsa hisses when she sees me. She is busy admiring her beauty while Aunt Lola growls and is constantly hungry. What they do not know is the fact that I am also constantly hungry and in the future, I won't accept anything from them when it comes to food.

The more I see, the more I purposefully walk through all the rooms. I run up and down the stairs and bravely jump from the couch to the carpeted floor. In general: Jumping and clowning around is funny. The staff either laughs or curses. I really don't understand why both react so differently.

🐻 Fun with the staff

5:20 AM: I wake up with violent capers on my staff's playground which they call a bed. Such nonsense! I finally bite into Mommy's toe. Why the hell is she screaming like that? Perhaps this has to do with the fact that some red paint is running down her toe after my bite. This is just revenge for last night when I was wrapped in the towel under vigorous protest and treated with the eye ointment again.

Twenty minutes later, my staff appears in the kitchen. There is a proper breakfast. Of course I also take some of my aunts. They are already big. I have to grow up and get my strength, so food in any form will be of value to me. If my bowl is empty, I just need to go to their bowls and growl softly. Then they'll get scared and run away, even though they are so much bigger than me. But I'm brave!

And now this damn tube comes again. The contents burn my eyes insanely.

Well, into the bathroom again to kill plenty of towels. They always hang so threatening from top to bottom and literally wait to be dragged from the towel rail.
So I strongly bite into them and pull them downwards until they lie flat on the ground.

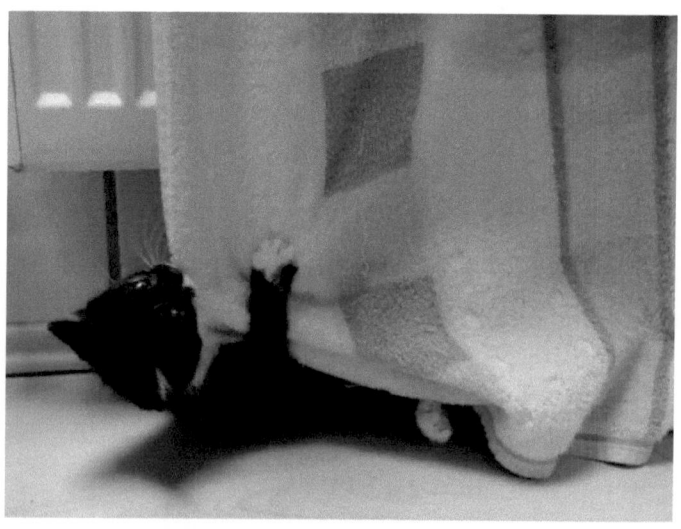

If Mommy and Daddy are also in the bathroom, it is quite possible that a towel is brought back to life and hangs over me, but now I have developed a completely well functioning technology to kill them by working my talons to pull a bunch of threads out of them.

My staff do not like that and then complain regularly about me, so they quickly bury the towels into the laundry basket mausoleum. Shortly thereafter, however, new towels reappear and I must kill them again quickly, before there are too many.
Such an uncontrolled proliferation of towels.

Meanwhile, I've discovered that I can pull a lot of different threads out of the carpet in the living room. As usual the staff cries out again when I do that, but carpets as well as towels and slippers also have to be immediately killed by me.

🐾 New Friends

Apparently today is a special day because quite a lot of people come to visit.

"Look Willy, here are Nadja and Steve, who come from far away because they have to pick up a tomcat from the farm and take it to their home, where their four cats already live. In addition, our friend Victoria, who also has four cats at home, is visiting, and wants to see you too, so behave yourself."

Pick up a tomcat? Me?
Help me, I don't want to go away from here!

But all is clear: I hear that they have brought over the little cat called Jerry. He previously lived on a farm somewhere in the 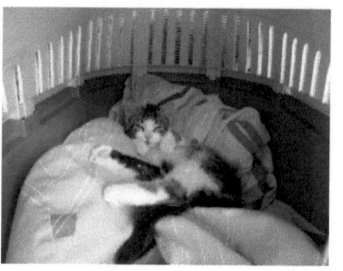 village. Now I also finally know who stole my personal litter box which is no longer in the kitchen anymore.

Jerry currently lives in my staff's summer house and without my knowledge and approval, they also provided him with my very own private toilet.

Well, the aunts also have a toilet on the first floor and even if they know nothing of his good fortune; this one is now using my private property. The other cat is finally leaving today and will be going on a long journey with his new staff and will then get his own toilet at the new destination.

I would like to get to know Jerry, but Mommy and Daddy say that I can't go out because I'm still so tiny and cannot see properly yet. Actually, that's mean. All are sitting in the garden and having fun in the glorious weather while I have to stay in the house.

Anyway, it is terribly exciting. So many new faces and they all look so incredibly nice.

All they say is how sweet and pretty I am.
I am cuddled and petted all the time. No one
is wrapping me in a towel and treating my
eyes with ointment against my will.
Everyone is spoiling me to their heart's
content.

Maybe I should take a ride and visit Jerry or
Victoria's other cats. Eventually they will be
nicer to me and won't snarl and growl at me
all day, just as the aunts constantly do.

A few days of vacation would perhaps not be so bad as I've heard Victoria whisper that she wants to steal me because I'm supposed to be so sweet.

She even says that to Daddy and Mommy and they laugh. They jokingly say that she can do this if she likes daily bloody hands and calves and that she should definitely get a large bottle of disinfectant and a large pack of bandages ready.

After Jerry's departure, my private toilet, as if by magic, was back in the kitchen. I think that's really good, now I have two toilets, where I can make new desert planets and Daddy can search for this famous *'spice'* between the sandworms.

🐾 Up with the left paw

5:30 AM: I have slept far away from the staff's alarm clock.

Well, I'll look for breakfast and then think about how mischievous I can be today. So down to the kitchen I go. This is  just too much: Aunt Lola is sitting in my private toilet and growls at me.

"I do not want to share my feed with dis littel black devil," she grumbles and leaves the kitchen indignantly with a loud growling.

As if this is not enough, the staff comes again with this awful eye ointment and wrap me back into this hated towel. This is so frustrating and as compensation I will now go into the bathroom and kill at least one of those disgusting towels, although Daddy and Mommy always find this so funny and laugh a lot about it.

There is less laughter when I go to the bathroom and leave pretty sand dunes on the floor.

Daddy says enervated each time, *"Yeah, your private bathroom attendant is almost there, who cleans up the mess and is now searching for the 'spice'. Besides, you smell like five adult cats. If you were on the toilet, that would be almost unbearable!"*

So my sand dunes are beautiful and by the way: Daddy also really stinks quite a lot.

My left eye has now healed nicely and I can see quite well with it. On the right side, everything still looks quite cloudy. This does not matter. With half my vision, I still manage to bite unerringly into Mommy's big toe. Funny, that she always cries and says to Daddy that he should quickly stop the blood. Oh, just calm down, those are just my tiny little milk teeth. They hardly hurt at all.

🐾 The early bird catches the worm

I've learned to read the clock and of course I can use this for my own purpose.

5:06 AM: It is the ideal time for waking up the staff. They bring me something new. It is a funny bouncy castle, which is about 5.9 feet wide and 6.5 feet long, beautifully padded and solely intended for my personal use only. They call it a bed, but this cannot be true, because a bed is more than twelve inches tall and has a round shape. I know this because I always sleep there at night.

 However, what bothers me, is the fact that the staff get up early in the morning. My bouncy castle has tipped over. Now I have to get them up anyway, so I will have more space for my capers.

Well, I jump from Mommy's foot into her face who then at the next moment hits the back of her head into Daddy's face and she cries out. This constant crying and whining is really annoying. Staff nowadays is really very sensitive.

In any case, now I have space to run around, because Daddy and Mommy get up and I have my playground to myself.

Hunger drives me into the kitchen, where the aunts are also waiting. Yes, food is still something so nice and especially what the aunts have in their bowls.

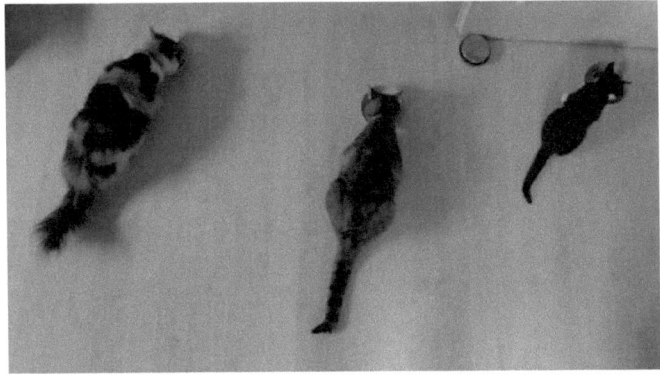

After Molly, Salsa and Lola have already eaten, they are finally outside. Good food should not go to waste and Daddy says
"The little one still needs to grow."
I have grown more than 300 grams in the last two weeks.

Why do the aunts go angrily outside now? Only because I nibbled a little of their food? This does not matter as I'm tired and now I have to take a nice long digestive sleep.

If my staff is tired, I could eliminate the toy box and play with these funny balls with bells inside. They make nice noises when you push them across the floor and when they fall down the stairs. When night falls, I'm usually good and voluntarily go into my bed. Of course, mostly before that, I need to test my bouncy castle as to whether the staff are playing dead again.

They are usually always mean and throw me out of my playground. This expulsion takes about ten seconds and then when I reclaim my bouncy castle again. Then the game starts all over again until I'm really tired. I crawl back into my bed, begin purring and suckle on the washing label. This method helps me to fall asleep really fast so that I have more strength for the next day.

5:30 AM: Time to wake up the staff, and today with a very perfidious method.

After I practice leapfrog in my bouncy castle and just because the staff have no business being here, I quietly creep under the quilt and bite into Mommy's toe. Yes, the night's sleep is now over, although the alarm keeps ringing for another hour.

Why are people constantly screaming? Well, at first it's time to take flight and play on the floor with my bell ball, so this makes funny noises in the morning. After the initial excitement has settled and the staff tries to sleep five more minutes, I once again practice the *'jump into Mommy's face'*. Today this works because her defensive measures are not quite as good as yesterday.

The next morning, I get up before the alarm clock rings. 5:00 AM is always a good time to run around in my bouncy castle, bearing in mind that all the bed springs make a noise and the slatted frames are creaking so as to entertain the staff.

🖋 Weekend

Mommy and Daddy are maundering about someone who is called *'Weekend'* or something that I do not know about. Just as they seem to complain about it not being nice because they constantly say it. Ironically, it must be the *'Weekend'*, so I've decided to abolish this *'Weekend'*. I think this is a good idea and they will certainly be very grateful to me for it, if this *'Weekend'* does not come.

It usually always pleases me when I strongly jump onto the face of Mommy, who is not yet fully awake. It is the right beginning for the day.

Thereupon she starts to yell and jumps out of my bouncy castle to treat the bloody scratches just next to her eye with alcohol. She goes without my further request into the kitchen because my aunts are already waiting with loud penetrating singing, as if they have received nothing to eat for at least three days.

Breakfast! My own food? Yuck! Of course my aunts' food tastes much better. So I head towards the bowl with a roar. I don't hear their growling. In addition, Aunt Molly is a picky eater and is leaving her bowl early, so it would be a pure waste to let the food spoil.

Aunt mostly leaves the house early in the morning because she prefers to use her toilet in the 'nature'. She told me that it is huge and has plenty of space for scratching. Unfortunately, my staff has forbidden me to view this nature toilet with the words, *"You'll have to wait a little longer until you are allowed to go out."*

Maybe I should learn how to open doors?

Oh crap, now the staff comes again with this cursed eye ointment and wrap me in the towel which I hate so much. So I start screaming, growling and fighting, but I can't fight it. It's of no advantage as they still bring the ointment every day!

By the way, my hind legs are held under the tap, because I did a round of Charleston in my private litter box after the 'big business' and I left corresponding tracks throughout the house.

"Willy, you're not a cat, but a litterbug and whoever stinks and is so dirty like you, has to be washed!"

They still have not figured out that I can wash myself only at a time when I decide to.

In protest, I have joined the 'Occupy Basket Movement' and cheekily occupy Aunt Molly's sleeping place in the bathroom. They don't know where they can withdraw to, when I annoy them.

Otherwise, the usual morning: Salsa into the house, Lola out of the house. Molly cannot decide where she really wants to be and I have to stay at home anyway.

🐾 Swimsuits are for wimps

People are sometimes strange, they need a bathroom to clean themselves.
For me it's easy: I sit down somewhere, lick myself from front to back and the laundry is already done.

With my staff it's so funny and I always have to watch what they're doing in the bathroom. They really wet themselves from top to bottom with water that I always drink when I'm thirsty.

When they are finished, they take the towels I have killed and rub themselves with them. I usualy test whether people are really dry and at the same time run my claws on Mommy's calf until it bleeds again. She then screams while she wipes the blood.

After I checked the condition of her skin, I climb up the Mount laundry basket over the narrow heating edge onto the bath tub Valley, which is as white as deep snow. *"Willy, we have summer and don't live at the North Pole, the tub looks always like this."* My staff begins to laugh.

Aunt Molly sits under a silver thing and is fluttering the ripple-dipple that comes up there. Is that dangerous? It would be better to have two feet safety distance when it makes this sounds again and slurp off the ground when it stops. Aha, that's also water on my feet and I do not like that.

🐾 Games without frontiers

The next day at 4:15 AM, this strange jingle sounds again. My staff calls it an alarm clock. So clearly today is too early for me, because yesterday, I was fooling around so much that I needed twenty minutes to get going to extensively test the bouncy castle.

Breakfast! Who needs to get to the bowl first? Me, of course, because otherwise I turn into a beast! Aunt Lola and Aunt Molly feed peacefully. Aunt Salsa comes in delayed as usual because she is so beautiful and feeds on the window sill. She is quite the supposed aristocrat.

Finished with food? Well then, let's get out of the door. Anyway only the aunts leave because they are already grown up. I will now sort out a shoebox and rip the wrapping paper contained therein.

This crackling sound is so wonderful when you dishevel it into thousand parts and decorate half the living room floor. It seems to be truly more comfortable now. The whole area is garnished with balls and fabric mice and you've got a pretty neatly decorated living room.

Now as my staff is finally awake and busy with cleaning and clearing up, I can nap on the yet to be scratched carpet, and think about how I can go on clowning around for the rest of the day.

Revenge! Just because I raged in my private bouncer at half past twelve at night without ceasing and then hacked my claws in Daddy's toes, I will get thrown out?

Why does the staff still need to sleep? Daddy can't still be tired! As a consequence, they have closed the bedroom door without my permission and Molly's basket in the bathroom has to serve as a place for me to sleep.

Oh, how boring, there's no one to tease here because Aunt Molly's allowed to stay in the bedroom and the other two aunts are on the impossibly tall cabinet in the living room. Oh, is it so dreary! Maybe I should 'clean up' the living room a little?

Such a bedroom prohibition can do wonders. I have behaved pretty decently almost the whole day and in the evening there is freshly grilled chicken as a reward.

Unfortunately, my staff does not have the camera ready because every piece of chicken is eaten by me with a benevolent growl and they laugh the whole time.

I think chicken will be my favourite dish in the future, although my aunts tell me that warm mouse and fresh bird is by far more delicious.

People are sometimes really funny:
Either they laugh when I am raging through the area, play games with balls or have fun with my aunts or they scream quite terribly if I spoil them tenderly with my claws and teeth and sweep things such as mobile phones and cameras off the table in order to have more space for me.

🐾 The bowl is not enough

A new morning dawns and all goes well. I do not get the dreaded eye ointment, but Daddy puts a long white thing in my mouth.

"Today there will be a change of plan. You will get a parasitic treatment, little man," and he squeezes on the end of this thing.

Do I get this *'spice'* now? Ugh, this crap tastes horrible, yuck! *"Never fear, this one you will only get every two weeks."* However, this is a small consolation and as a consequence Aunt Molly and Aunt Lola must be annoyed until they disappear outside quite enervated. Good side effect: There is still some breakfast left.

As usual Aunt Salsa is sleeping as if in a coma at this time and there is also another change to my program: Slippers aren't killed immediately, but guarded, because they smell from time to time like Daddy's old, worn socks, which I like so much.

 Tonight is quite funny and I kindly tell my staff that they have to go to sleep when I freely go into my basket.

So I turn off the bedroom TV with the remote and close the door; a set of powerful front paws is sufficient for such actions.

Why the heck is the staff now laughing in the dark? For this, I will now walk into my basket and suckle myself to sleep.

🐾 Sleep in?

The staff could sleep in, but:

- 🐾 4:00 AM:
- 🐾 Floor exercises with following dodge bally.
- 🐾 5:30 AM:
- 🐾 Open the bouncy castle and kill some towels.
- 🐾 6:00 AM:
- 🐾 Thrown out of the bedroom, but the kitchen is transformed into a battlefield, as determined at 8:00 AM.
- 🐾 9:15 AM:
- 🐾 Weekly weigh-in with the result, that my weight is now two pounds.
- 🐾 9:30 AM:
  Hectic transporting of some scrunchies between living room and kitchen ...

Why does my staff actually look so tired?

Today, even the morning is miraculous:
Breakfast with Aunt Molly and Aunt Lola
without the usual bitching and growling.
Early in the morning, Aunt Salsa is basically
still in her coma.

What? Just Antibiotics? No eye ointment?
Finally this *'wrap-into-a towel'* drama ends
and I can kill some linen in a more relaxed
attstate.

🐾 Gifts everywhere!

Tonight I receive a letter, which is so exciting!

Why do I get mail? It's simple:
Daddy and Mommy run around continuously with this thing in their hands, which makes very quiet click sounds. When they press a button, sometimes, for a moment it is awfully bright. The people call it a camera and what they do with it, is called photography.

Then they take photos of me and send them into a box, which is called the Internet or something. A lot of other people, who also have cats or who like cats, can see the photos of me or photos of other cats.

It looks as if I have received quite a good feedback and many people like me because I have already received three packages from a Jutta, a Jenny and a Jasmine.

So it seems that I do leave a permanent impression on people whose name begins with a 'J'. Although they all live quite far away from here, they have informed me that they want to visit me one day.

Inside the package, are all great things for me: Treats, a red heart that smells really nice like old worn socks and Jutta's rustle tunnel. In addition, there is still some canned food inside the boxes. However, they are not all for me but also for the cats at the farm where I was found.

My aunts also received gifts; which are small pillows that also smell like worn old socks. People call it valerian and turn up their noses at it, but my Aunts and I are really addicted to this stuff. We all then play with our pillows, toss and overturn them on the floor.

Daddy photographs everything and Mommy also suddenly has a camera in her hand and films us while she giggles:

"Now our kittens are totally stoned. We have a bunch of drug addicts at home."

They then all laugh, including us. This is the first real party in my life and of course I could get used to it.

Out of sheer joy, I attack my rustling tunnel and forget that I have to pee. This is really quite embarrassing for me because the whole tunnel rather looks like a small mountain lake and my staff just laugh at me.

I am indeed sure that this will not happen to me again, but after two days at exactly 6:01 AM and another dose of valerian, my tunnel has to be washed again and dried in the sun.

Comment from the staff:
"That's what happens when you get your first trip early in the morning."

Today I have my first wake-up call at 7:00 AM because it's Sunday and I still feel the after effects of this valerian.

For a change, Lola hisses all morning and Molly and Salsa have fled outside.

Aunt Molly always comes back first and knocks at the screen door with her paw for our staff to let her in immediately.

 My mountaineering skills have improved so much. I can now reach the dining table summit plateau of the Mount Kitchen Chair and I make it to the cosy Valle le Fruit Basket.

I've also discovered a new fun game. It is called: 'kitchen table up, kitchen table down' and it goes like this:

I climb on the table; my staff yells
"Get off immediately!"
They grab me and put me on the floor and then
I climb back up again. This only gets boring
when I do it twenty to thirty times or when the
yelling gets on my nerves. I then prefer to take
a walk into the living room to pull out some
carpet threads.

🐾 Criminal tango

The staff can sleep in late.
The staff cannot sleep late.
7:15 AM:
A slap in the stairwell, silence ...

 Mommy jumps out of bed as if bitten by a tarantula to see what has happened and calls Daddy to also jump out of bed. He drags himself down on all fours and grumbles.

A crime must have happened. There are three drops of blood on the tiled floor which point in the direction of the living room. Who wanted to attack who and throw who down the stairs? Daddy first brings some kitchen roll, eliminates traces of blood as he finds them, drags himself grumbling on all fours back to bed and murmurs:

"Mommy will clean up the mess in the kitchen later, I'm still too tired."

As it turns out, I have a slight minor injury on my chin, but I cannot remember what happened. I just know that I recently played with my valerian heart and then probably had a blackout. Also, I remember a few white paws in front of me, which were either from Aunt Molly, Aunt Salsa or perhaps my own?

Maybe we should ask the village policeman Caruso. After all, he knows almost everyone from this place, because he has his roots everywhere.

Actually, he is an aria singer by profession. He has since moved away from his old home at the vets because of a dog who strays around the area. This dog knows all the garages, stables and sofas in the region.

Thus, a well-travelled cat might help to elucidate the sinister deed. But as it's always the case, just this morning Caruso is once again nowhere to be found. Presumably he is just in front of another door and smashes an Italian aria called 'O sole meow' because he is constantly hungry.

Well, that's enough of a sleep in for the two legged creatures. In my opinion they've slept enough for today.

I hear Mommy say,

"Now we need to clarify whether the early action was a cowardly attack done by the aunts or just messing around by a half-grown little devil."

Daddy says,

"He simply gets up to too much nonsense in the morning," before I retire back into my basket and take another snooze.

What really happened, nobody will know, because my staff is a bit stupid and does not understand my language. Although they have a dictionary in the cupboard *'Cat-English', 'English-Cat,'* I don't really think that they seriously understand what I meow to them.

To make matters worse, they're also back in my private bouncy castle and play dead.

Is this another criminal case or are they just tired? I'll go and see if they are still alive and bite them gently into their toe or earlobe.

🖋 Colour Capriccio

What is going on again today? Daddy has almost cleared out the whole kitchen and brought out a large bucket filled with white coloured water. But whenever I want to know how the water tastes, he says to me: *"Willy, go away from the wall colour, this is not for you!"* That's so mean, I just want to try it, but he will not let me.

In addition to the bucket, there is a piece of wood attached with whiskers and a round furry animal that looks like a small drum. But I think the animal is dead, because it does not move when I touch it.

"Willy, this is a brush and a paint roller. Go away before you have all the paint on your feet; they are white enough."

Now he dives this furry animal into the wall colour and it is literally drowned in it. Oh, I have to control that everything is above board and watch my breadwinner all day while painting. But I think it's much more interesting and funny that I help Daddy. *"Willy, go away from the wall, otherwise you will have all the paint colour in your fur and on the paws."*

I think Daddy sees this completely wrong. I just want the kitchen looking a bit nicer and not so boring. It is much more creative when I decorate the floor in an artful way with paw prints and seriously; who has such an artistic kitchen floor? Solid maple is really boring and my artwork also has the 'side effect' that you can't see any crumbs from the last breakfast.

Granted, I run a few times crosswise and apply a little too much pattern, but Daddy constantly wipes my road with a wet rag and destroys my painstakingly created works of art. At some point I'll make it but have to leave a lasting impression in the truest sense of the word.

I then decorate the living room couch with some of my autographs, but Daddy is not amused and he comments, *"Good thing the colour is soluble in water when it's noticed immediately"* and he is sweating terribly.

Oh yes, as for the sweating, I like that. The people always have an interesting smell under their armpits and I could sniff it for hours. Aunt Molly taught me this, but she smells something else that is called perfume.

She told me if Daddy comes home, his neck smells so incredibly interesting that she has to lick his head.

He tells her: *"Molly, I sprayed my neck with the most expensive perfume at the Perfumery, so that you have something to sniff and lick."*

I'd also like to smell it sometimes but he does not lift me up as high as Aunt Molly, because I scratch and bite. I bit his upper lip twice already which gave him a bit of a scar.

Mommy and Daddy don't understand this. Sometimes I can only wonder if I would be suitable as a tattoo artist. After all, I have already scratched some wonderful tattoos on Mommy's nose and calves and on Daddy's upper lip and ear.

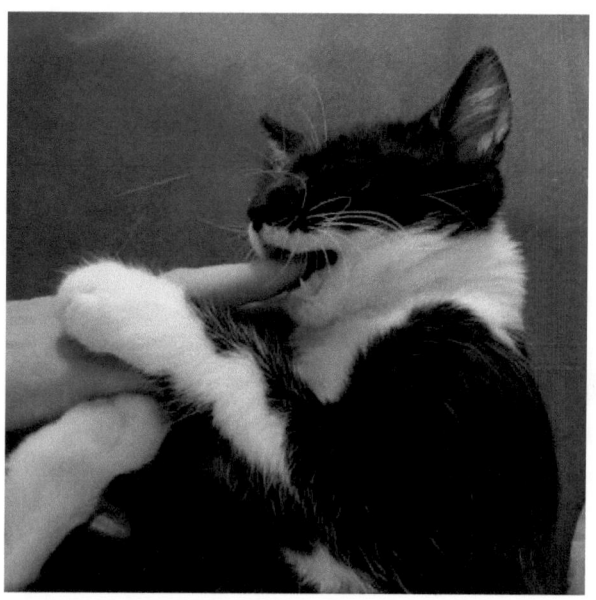

🪶 Morning exercises

2:00 AM: Aunt Molly finally comes home. It's a reason for me to go down to the kitchen with her and look for food. By the way, I find this toy again, with which I am able to noisily paint while enjoying the nocturnal silence.

4:30 AM: Floor exercises, of course with the appropriate volume for the early time of day.

6:15 AM: Visit to the bouncy castle with a cheerful calf bite.

6:30 AM: The staff is finally up. I am very hungry and must be fed first, otherwise there will be serious cases of petty theft. Also, I eat everything my aunts like or dislike. Reason enough for my aunts to leave the house as quickly as possible.
Direct quote from Aunt Lola: *"Dis littöl bläck deviil is costing mee my last nörves!"*

Well, then I'll just wear replacement hair bands and carry balls through the area.

This rustle I've been given, still gives me much joy, especially early in the morning when everyone else is still asleep and I can make funny noises with it.

In addition to the openings of the front and rear, there is a hole in the middle where I can jump into with full force across the living room floor. At the ends, there are small cords that are ideal to haul the tunnel from one room to another.

I usually carry the rustle to places where my staff may stumble over it. Guaranteed they will again begin to curse me in private. If they curse me, they don't seriously really mean it.

I'm really happy that my aunts don't care about my rustle because I can hide my whole prey, at least four hair bands, a crocheted mouse named Jutta, my valerian heart from Jasmin, various balls and a striped plush fish, in order to let them go again and disappear under some pieces of furniture.

🐾 Tombola

Last time my staff gave me a new gift called 'Cat Racetrack'. It was a round thing with a ball in it which only moved when you pushed it a little with the paw. Frankly, it was so boring because you couldn't even take out the ball. I lost interest in it. Anyway, I think that the ball was already dead.

There's nothing quite like Mommy's hair bands that I can hide anywhere in the house.

Because I didn't like this Racetrack anymore and as my aunts also showed no particular interest in it, my staff came up with the idea of giving the thing away to my fan club on the Internet.

Daddy folded a lot of little slips of paper with names on it and I was able to draw out the winner with my claws. He also took a photo so that all my fans could see that I drew the lot all by myself.

A certain Felicitas won the Racetrack and she wrote on the Internet that their cats were first afraid of it. They must be quite some wimps; nobody fears a dead ball.

I notice that my ears start to itch and I do not know why I constantly have to scratch them. Mommy and Daddy have somehow noticed it and put me into this weird little basket with a grid.

I don't like this at all. I am again taken to the vet. Fortunately, she lives just a few doors down the path which is actually quite nice. She explains to me that I have mites in my ears and then brushes them really clean with a liquid and long cotton swab.

It is not so pleasant, but afterwards my ears no longer itch and at least this time I am not being poked in the back.

As clean as my ears are now, I still will only hear properly when I want to and not when my staff talks to me.

🪶 Political education

Aunt Molly has a little basket in the bathroom. Aunt Salsa and Aunt Lola have baskets in the living room and what do I have, apart from a basket full of toys, a basket in the bedroom and a basket in the living room? Nothing! This has to change so I'm going to occupy all the beds belonging to my aunts in a coup.

Mommy says, *"Be careful that there is no fight with your aunts who do not like it if their beds are occupied"* and Daddy says shortly thereafter, *"Well, little kittens have to learn a lot, even this, which is called ranking."*

They then published on the Internet that I invented the *'Occupy Bed Movement'* and told me that there are already a lot of avid followers. From all parts of the world, cats have joined the movement to occupy not only baskets but also tables, chairs, sofas, beds and bellies and legs belonging to their staff.

 In the name of solidarity, I'm so nice and alternately fill the bowls belonging to all the aunts, so that they are treated equally by me.

I should think about whether I should start the 'International Cat Bowl Party' as more cats are connecting to my 'Movement'. After all, I've heard that there are about millions of cat owners in the whole world. I think the odds to be elected as the next President are not too bad.

My first action would be the abolition of VAT on cat food, cat litter and cat toys, as well as the introduction of a free and preferred medical treatment at the vet.

In case of the question of equality, I have to think carefully about the abolition of the tax on dogs, because anyway for over 2,000 years, cats have been the secret rulers on earth.

Unfortunately shortly afterwards, I fall down from the cupboard with Aunt Salsa's bed.

I therefore decide to have nothing more to do with politics because it's far too dangerous and I prefer to transfer into the film industry as a stunt cat.

🐾 Feeding of predators

Food is nice! But basically never enough! My efforts to educate the staff properly with the food award is hugely difficult.

They still haven't realised that I need to be fed a good amount of meat first and then my aunts may be supplied with their basic necessities. So I force out my vociferous meow and growl, letting them know the correct order with my claws and especially my vocal cords. And lo and behold, it works!

At last I steal one of these little food cans. Unfortunately at that moment, Daddy just turns on the camera and films my robbery. He and Mommy bend over with laughter and later tell me that they released the movie on the Internet at a site called YouTube and all the people there laughed too.

So you cannot really call it privacy when they release one of my movies without my consent.

Incidentally, in contrast to the aunts, I have the advantage that I can really devour everything that is edible.

Aunt Molly is constantly turning up her nose, because she does not get her beloved egg soufflè and Aunt Salsa leaves her food stand in a huff because she is not served first, as she is the fairest of them all.

Of course, I certainly sacrifice myself for the dish as it would be a shame to let the good food spoil.

Aunt Lola is put on a diet by the staff, because she is supposedly too fat and too lazy.

"I am not fat and layzii", she grumbles every time and Mommy comments:
"She still looks elsewhere for a place to eat at the neighbours property because she always comes home bigger and still shows up for dinner at home."

In general, Mommy admits that she, as for us cats, is quite a *'mother hen'*. I have no idea what this means, but it probably has to do with the fact that she calls out loudly and runs through the neighbourhood in the evening when Aunt Salsa and Aunt Lola have not yet come home. In between, she grabs Daddy and is armed with a flashlight outside to search for the aunts, while they run around everywhere between the other houses.

Mommy mostly calls after Aunt Lola, because she, of all the aunts, is usually outside the longest. She asks all the neighbours where her cats are. When she comes back unsuccessfully after what feels like an eternity, again after ten minutes, the game begins all over again.

Lola told me that she sits in a hedge and is deliciously amused when Mommy and Daddy walk past for the tenth time and call her name.

"I ave alwaiis to restrain laughtöör and do not moov," she giggles.

Some time later, she goes home because Mommy cannot sleep and is perpendicular in my bouncy castle. Every evening she says,

"This cats cost me my last nerves! Starting tomorrow, they will remain in the house, even if Salsa poops daily in front of the oven out of sheer frustration."

The next morning, all the aunts are back on the garden path.

🐾 The sophisticated lady and her business

My staff says that Aunt Salsa is really quite a bitch. Granted, she is very pretty with her three colours, the long coat and baggy trousers on the hind legs already, but so far I did not know that a cat can be so conceited. All day long you should pay homage to her beauty and constantly emphasise how pretty she is.

Mommy told me that she was born in France and raised up with some sheep. But she believes she is a great-granddaughter of the domestic cat of Louis XIV.

As dirty as though she sometimes comes home, I cannot believe that and I think then that she is just an ordinary farm kitty from the French Basque country.

As for the bitching, she makes a woman like Naomi or someone like that, serious competition: She can grumble, growl and mewl like no other. Once Daddy and Mommy combed her because she came home from outside with a bunch of barnacles in her coat, while she sounded like the start to a 'Formula 1 Race'.

In addition, she claims that this Choupette, that a Karl or so owns and allegedly has two maids, is not fit to hold a candle to her, when it comes to beauty.

"Choupette is only so famous because this Karl was previously famous and most people chase idols like lemmings," she says.

What are idols and lemmings and why are they also called Karl?

The staff can only stroke Aunt Salsa when she is really in a good mood or famished and this is the case after a maximum of five hours.

If she does not get her will, she is always in the way that my staff stumbles over her and curse her terribly. This method *'to be in the way'* is really funny and if I do that, they curse me also.

Daddy and Mommy curse before breakfast when Aunt Salsa makes a smelly pile on the glass plate in front of the oven in the living room, only because she cannot leave the house early in the morning. When the staff does not immediately respond, she even makes a little yellow pudle that partially runs under the glass plate. The sun makes such beautiful light reflections on it and it sure does not smell like perfume.

Then she proceeds back into her basket with an uplifted tail and aspirates dryly:

"That's the deal."

🐾 Diet?

Aunt Lola is greedy, that's for sure. Well, I'm not just someone with a stomach as small as a mouse, but at least I have the excuse that I have to grow big and strong.

From dawn to dusk you can hear her make noises and she pretends that her stomach growls. Whenever there is breakfast, lunch or dinner, she comes and complains that she has received nothing for three days.

If Daddy or Mommy go into the kitchen, she immediately follows them because there could be something edible for her there.

She simulates a terrible growling stomach, relies on a suffering expression and constantly wiggles around the legs of the staff.

Sometimes this scam works for Mommy and she shares a round of crispies for all, because she says that no one should be discriminated.

If she is walking towards the kitchen and as I am quite capable of learning at my age, I take advantage of this and gallop after her. Although she complains every time and says: *"Get lost, you littel black Deviil,"* but I do not care because I'm constantly hungry too.

When Aunt Lola's at home and there is nohing to eat, she spends the rest of the time by growling and sleeping, while one of her feet is always hanging from the basket.
This is maybe a kind of signal that she wants to be left alone.

The other two aunts tell me that she is only active when she is outside in the garden. There, she catches pretty much everything with two or four legs, ie mice, rats and birds. Except for the rats, she devours everything that she catches and as an excuse, she then says that she gets nothing to eat at home and is on a diet.

However Mommy assumes that she has found a place somewhere in the neighbourhood, where she plays the role of a poor, hungry and oh so neglected cat and begs for a full cup of food. Therefore she comes home every day looking fatter.

Mommy now has the idea to mount a small camera around her neck, because she wants to know where Aunt Lola hangs out all day.

So, I do not mind this because I like to watch it all on this large square box, where everything moves around. Some funny sounds also come out of it. People call it a television. Moreover, it may well be possible that I may once go through the door, where the aunts always disappear from. If that's the case, then maybe I can also find out where the full food bowls in the neighbourhood are. I need not have to worry about my daily food supply.

After all, three bowls per day and the remains of my aunts are way too little to survive on.

🐾 Excursion with obstacles

Today is apparently a very special day. My staff runs excitedly through all the rooms, collect items of clothing and place them in a container with small wheels down below, which they call a suitcase.

In the bathroom they have wrapped up these little plastic things with short whiskers which they always put into in their mouth every morning and evening, moving them back and forth. They call these toothbrushes. Then they make such funny gurgling noises.

At an unobserved moment, I have tried what's on it and this doesn't taste so good. Aunt Molly likes it and on every occasion she smells and licks the foam remaining on Mommy's and Daddy's toothbrushes.

Suddenly I smell something special in the air. It is something that I only recognise when the house windows are open. I cannot get out because there is a very fine grid in front of it blocking my way out.

I've always wanted to know what is out there. Because I've only seen it from a distance, therefore I just follow this scent.

What's this? The door through which my aunts always disappear is usually closed and now it is open! As curious as I am, I dare myself to walk over the threshold behind Aunt Lola, who is already a few steps in front of me.

Oh, this is all interesting; loud noises and new things that I have never heard and seen before in my life. But as soon as I walk down the stairs, I hear the resolute voice of Mommy coming from the door: *"Who the heck left the door open. All the cats are gone and we were just about to leave!"*

Unfortunately, this was a short trip, because the next moment I'm lifted up and carried back into the house.

Shortly thereafter, Aunt Salsa is put back next to me and she starts to complain. After what feels like an eternity, Aunt Lola is back. My staff closes the door from the outside and tell me that Mommy has launched a search for her where she crawls through all the bushes in the garden and asks all the neighbours, who were up at seven o'clock on Saturday morning.

Aunt Lola does not understand all the fuss, because she is just sitting and waiting next to the front door behind a garbage can until she is finally brought back home.

Apparently my staff seems angry with us today because they have not yet come home. It becomes so late and when it is dark, there is no one in my bouncy castle to bite in the toes.

It is terribly boring, because all the aunts are just lying around and sleeping most of the time.

I am so bored that I eat everything in the bowls that are filled with lots of food, and then I fall asleep with a full belly.

 The next morning, there is still no one at home and the day is really boring. From time to time I look out of the window, where the iron sheet animal (car) belonging to my staff usually rolls back and forth, but there is nothing, absolutely nothing to see and hear.

Quite late in the evening, Mommy and Daddy return back home and are thrilled to see us.

My aunts and I are at first offended, because they left us alone for so long without our permission. Sulking works wonders and they immediately fill our bowls with chicken meat as an excuse for their guilt.

We are then quite gracious and forgive them after a handful of snacks.

🐾 Gourmet

I love noodles!
Today at noon my staff cooks noodles and of course I have to try them immediately as to whether they taste good.

It's really annoying that cats are not allowed on the kitchen table, but in this case I just cannot help to steal a single macaroni. What a treat, I'm totally thrilled. First I only suck it, but over time I realise that I can bite it properly as well and it tastes incredibly good.

Unfortunately there is almost nothing left on the plate and I have, apart from the four meat rations, to suffer terribly with hunger until the next day. There is one thinner and longer macaroni.

Actually it is called spaghetti, but I can't say that, if I just have one in my mouth.

Out of sheer greed I have to anchor my tender rear claws into Mommy's thigh to hit the trail even more. I have decided that I will no longer pay attention to her cries, when it comes to pasta. Most of the time she then runs off to disinfect her wounds and this is my chance to scrounge yet another noodle.

My staff says something about a hangover cat called Luigi and his cannelloni; but I think that's something completely different.

A few days later there is the next culinary delight for me, namely cakes. Now that's not quite as hearty as the pasta especially with a bit of tomato sauce, but it tastes quite good.

A Poundcake is sweet, tasty and filling, at least for humans. I'm not tired of it and need more, but eventually my staff's plates are empty again. There are such red moist pieces which people call strawberries, but I have not yet tasted them. When it comes to me, the staff could appear each day with a cargo of cake.

Meanwhile I have personally tested nearly everything that is edible on my staff's table. Finally, it could still happen, that a wonderful treat slips through my claws.

However, I soon realise that not everything that people eat is tasty, for example salted potato chips. This is totally disgusting and I cannot understand why my staff eats a whole bag of these.

For me the little cubes of Emmentaler are much tastier, because you can really chew on them. But as for these green beads, which are called grapes, she can eat herself because I do not like the taste of them anyway.

One of my new favourite dishes is boiled potatoes or fried potatoes. Because they taste so good, I've pilfered some directly from Mommy's fork. These long potato sticks, which are called 'fries' by the people, are also quite 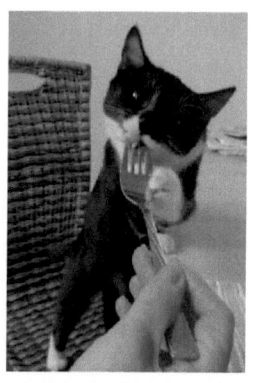 delicious and much easier to steal when Daddy or Mommy just aren't watching their plates.

I now only have to consider how I will manage to educate Daddy. Whenever I climb on the kitchen table, he calls: *"Get off the table immediately!"* It is difficult to obey, especially when it comes to these delicious chicken parts.

Whether I bravely climb up the chair without carabiners and safety line or use Mommy's thigh as a climbing aid, constantly on such occasions, this is a senseless clamor. Anyway I do not listen.

I grumble after him, but prefer to go down before I get any more pasta or chicken. It's really too bad that pasta, cakes or even better chicken are never on the table when my staff are not at home.

To make matters worse, they have now also locked all the little bags with the delicious meat specifically for us cats, into a plastic box, because I had eaten a few while they were not at home.

Yesterday Mommy was cooking baked zucchini with garlic and did not let me try it. Then when my staff briefly left the kitchen after dinner, it was my turn:

Because I have already grown quite a bit, I made a leap to the kitchen and opened the lid of the bowl, where the rest was inside. The meat and cheese tasted really good, however the garlic was not to my liking.

I was really naughty and a short time later for most of the night, I was lying on the couch with stomach ache. Somehow I had absolutely no desire to play with my aunts or annoy the staff. Mommy said it's not good if cats eat garlic and Daddy said that I still have to learn a lot.

I think he's right, because a week ago it was similar. I secretly stole these delicious chewing bars and guzzled down a part of the aluminum packaging. For the rest of the day the fun was gone and the next morning when I went to the bathroom, I released glitter sausages.

Daddy laughed and said
"This happens when you are greedy little beast."

I am hungry again!

🐾 Love games

Aunt Molly told me that she has a buddy named Caruso outside the house, with whom she goes out walking and together they like to catch mice. He is totally fascinated about Molly's *'Cindy Crawford beauty spot'* on her nose.

I would really like to get out and get to know him, but my staff thinks that I'm too small to explore the world and be left alone with strange cats. They said if some strangers talk to me, regardless whether cat or person, I should first of all run away quickly. This would be much safer.

Caruso is the local village policeman. He knows exactly where there's something to eat in the village where you can settle down with impunity on a couch or in a strange bouncy castle. He claims that he was born and raised at the Arena di Verona and that is why in addition to his career as a police officer, he is also a gifted opera singer.

During summer I have even heard him sing a few times at home, while the windows were open.

Honestly, he can sing really well, even though my staff thinks he sounds like he has a terrible hangover and wishes to blackmail them just because of food. Actually maybe everything is just a facade and he is a real Mafioso.

What Aunt Molly tells me is that he eats better than he can sing. He manages to eat complete feed bowl with 200 grams in less than twenty seconds, while he does not care what was in the cup nor the manufacturer.

A few years ago, due to circumstances that no one knows about, he was brought to the vet next door, where he had his sleeping place in the waiting room next to the counter. He then welcomed the new patients, including their staff with a serenade from his repertoire and had fun during the waiting time with them.

Last year, the vet took on a young dog, called Labrador and Caruso did not like him at all. After his protests were simply ignored, he packed his belongings and moved out.

Since then, he roams from house to house in the village and thus knows all the surrounding garages, barns, sheds and loopholes. A few doors down from here, he has reserved a couch, which he shares with two pugs. Since he's there, the pugs have nothing to report, because he has told them clearly that from now on he alone is the boss.

Since then, the pugs always run excitedly to the garden fence whenever people pass by and act like large mastiffs. Most people just laugh and say how cute the two doggies are. At the pug owners, the gourmet menu for Caruso is dry food only and is quite sparely stocked. Therefore he is outside our door very often and gives Aunt Molly one of his best Italian arias. She likes the songs very much and they nudge each other at their noses.

Previously, Molly did not want to have anything to do with him, but over time she realised that he actually is really nice. In front of the other two aunts he is a bit scary, probably because he cannot speak French.

If Daddy does not respond immediately and presents something edible next to the doorstep, Caruso clearly means *"You give molto Mangiare for Patrone pronto, otherwise I have to sing the whole day."*

My staff then responds fairly quickly by satisfying the hunger of the singer. Afterwards they think that Caruso, with his blackmailing methods, must be somewhere from Sicily.

Once he has guzzled down all the food, he usually goes without a word of thanks and warps with Aunt Molly inside the next best hedge.

Molly told me in confidence that they only cuddle because both are no longer able to mate and Caruso has a daughter from a previous relationship. So really I do not understand it and she said: *"You'll understand soon enough."*

So really, I have finally come to an age where I should at least be informed of some basic things, but every time I address the subject of cat and cat with Aunt Molly, she avoids me and meows with inconsequential spells, just like Aunt Salsa and Aunt Lola.

In fact, she lives quite withdrawn and when she's home, she usually goes to the bathroom, where her basket is or spreads out on my bouncy castle. She is now more often back in the living room on the couch and sleeps there. For some time she no longer trusts anyone, because the other two aunts have claimed the living room for themselves and she is pretty scared because of the aunts' hissing. Since then, the situation has somewhat eased.

As I have just learned, Aunt Lola is now in love head over heels. She made friends out there with an unknown black and white cat, who is apparently drawn back here. This is probably the reason why she always comes home later and Mommy is therefore regularly on the verge of a nervous breakdown. In any case, Lola is much more balanced and always has this glorified look as if she is hiding out with her new boyfriend. However, she is absolutely not quite so glorified when the staff decides that she cannot go out for the day. She then sits at the locked front door totally disgruntled and growls like crazy.

In frustration she then stuffs everything edible that she can find and tries to beat up Aunt Molly. There is always a huge outcry because the staff also vigorously screams too, but in the end nothing becomes of it, because we cats cannot even open doors.

Specifically, when a key must be turned in the door, we have no chance at all and a cat flap where you could whim in and out, is also not there. Daddy used to have a cat that could open all doors. This annoyed him so much in the long run, that he then turned all the keys around everywhere.

Aunt Salsa has decided that she currently likes to remain alone and wants to focus entirely on her beauty. In France, she gave birth to three kittens and then separated from her 'lover' because she was just too beautiful for anyone.

All day long she walks around with her bushy tail raised up and presents her fancy harem pants on the hind legs. When she sees me, she starts to growl and says: *"I do not need a mirror on the wall, I even know that I am the fairest of them all."*
It's no surprise to me that she has no boyfriend, because in the long run, no cat could really stand such incredible bitching.

Mommy told me in confidence that she is always secretly hanging out with the neighbourhood sheep because she grew up in France with lots of sheep.

Well, they are probably so stupid as to believe her tales with the castle, the many white horses and the Sun King.

She is such a diva; all the sheep bleat in agreement and find it great. Daddy said that, moreover, with people this is also quite often the case.

Love seems to be something beautiful.

I sometimes listen to the aunts' stories when they come back home. That seems not only to be with us as cats, but also for the people when I sometimes hear strange noises coming from my bouncy castle. Every time a sign hangs on the door and reads, *'The bouncy castle is closed during maintenance'*. I don't think so, because the noises do not sound like work.

Maybe I have to come of age to understand what love really means. Currently I rather prefer fabric mice, plastic balls and hair ties as toys.

🐗 Gifts again!

This morning, I sat at the window and was daydreaming. This yellow car came again down to near the front of my house. A man got out, opened the rear door and hauled out two huge packages.

Shortly thereafter, there was a mooing at the door and my aunts and I first hid from these comical sounds. Later, Mommy informed me that Daddy programmed the doorbell with a 'cow mooing' sound, because he was bored with normal bells.

We cats are scared of this noise every time. In my and Mommy's opinion, it is time that Daddy programmes a new sound in the door bell.
I would for example like *'Ode to joy'* or even *'I hear you knocking.' It* would be better than this nerving and loud mooing, which scares us all.

Daddy then replies, *"Haha, the next time I will program 'Hells Bells' into it."*

After I calm down, I crawl out from under my bouncy castle and walked into the living room, where those big yellow boxes are situated. Of course at first I have to examine the contents thoroughly before my staff can unpack everything.

The packages came from far away up north from Anja, who also has cats at home. She often saw pictures of me on the Internet. Because she apparently likes me, she sent a lot of gifts to me, my staff and the cats from the farm, where I was found as a kitten.

At the top there is a sealed letter. Because I'm still so tiny and cannot read and write, I meow to Mommy that she should read the letter to me.

Anja wrote that the first packet is meant for me, my aunts and my staff and the second package is for the farm cats. She also wrote that she sent the packages as a thank-you to us for the many beautiful photos and stories about me and the farm cats which my staff put onto the Internet with the story about how they had saved my life back then.

The letter is of course in my fan mail drawer which Mommy and Daddy reserved especially for me. In the package for the farm cats are lots of canned food, bags of meat and those delicious thin stalks which all the cats usually only get as a reward. I could actually cram myself in there all day.

I immediately steal one of them and in no time squash it so that no one can take it away from me.

 Later I secretly steal one of these stalks from the package, but I forget that you can't eat the packaging. That's why I feel really unwell for the rest of the day. I have no desire to mess around and trouble my staff anymore with my activities.

Daddy and Mommy quickly put the package outside so I cannot steal more and ruin my stomach. Later after I do my *'big business'*, I am feeling fine again.

The real surprise however, is in the second package!

For Daddy and Mommy there are chocolates and candies, and I would like to try them, but they say that is toxic to cats.

For me and my aunts there are these excellent snacks packed with cheese, which you can only get when you're really good. Anyway, I prefer them to silly chocolate, which only makes me feel sick.

But on the very bottom of the package there is still something great which is wrapped in gift paper and I cannot not wait for my staff to unpack this special gift.

I'm curious and quite restless until Mommy finally opens the paper. The content is a great pillow with a photo of me printed on it. My staff and I are amazed and we all are really pleased.

My pillow then gets a place of honour in the living room next to Aunt Salsa's pillow. She is always so conceited; thinks she has one extra pillow. She is probably not amused as now I have one too. I do not care, I find my pillow beautiful and everyone else finds that too.

🐾 Farm cats

Daddy and Mommy head off and bring the gift package from Anja to the farm, where all the other cats are very happy over the delicious contents.

Usually they only get dry food, but during milking time, fresh cow's milk is served. They usually always have to get breakfast, lunch and dinner by themselves by catching mice and rats. That's why they rejoice with the welcoming change of diet.

One day my staff told me who lives out there on the farm:

Mr. Skewhead is the head of the farm cats and has ruled for about ten years now. He has a lot of turf wars behind him and looks very bold with his bitten ears and lack of teeth. Nevertheless, he is a very nice cat who likes to cuddle with people. A straw bale probably fell on his head many years ago which is why he has such a funny name.

Mrs. Basedow is one of his wives and her trademark is her bushy tail, which is usually smeared with cowpie because she always runs across the cowshed. She likes to cuddle up to people, who too then also smell like cowpie.

When Daddy and Mommy return from the farm, they also always heavily smell like cowpie.

Mr. Rötli is a distinguished and reserved cat, who indeed likes some stroking, but then wants to be left alone again. He usually looks for a warm place in the sun in order to spend the day sleeping.

He has a very shaggy, but still well-groomed coat. Many other cats envy him because during the winter, he doesn't freeze so fast like them.

Franzi is two years old and one of the younger farm cats. Although she is extremely thin and delicate, she still is very sturdy and tough. Being a very small cat, she once had a heavy cold for a long time and was busy sneezing all day long.

Meanwhile, she's really healthy, because the vet checks her from time to time at the farm and she also gets her medication. Whoever strokes Franzi has problems to get rid of her, because she is so affectionate.

Luigi is a young, naughty, red furred cat of Italian descent who just thinks of *'Amore'* the whole day long. He believes that he can eventually replace Mr. Skewhead as the boss and then wants to start a *'Bunga-Bunga Republic'*.

Mr. Skewhead has however noticed his intention and recently gave him a warning by scratching him on the ear, causing some blood to draw. Since then Luigi has retreated somewhat but turned out really nice and can also now be caressed.

Herzibobbele is a nice cat and everyone likes him because of his heart-shaped nose.

Initially he was very shy, but Mommy always brought him a few treats on their visits and he became more and more trusting.

Meanwhile, he can be caressed from time to time and runs behind the staff when they leave the farm.

Besides there are also Isabelle, Mrs. Slurrydump and a few other cats who are usually somewhere in the bushes or hiding elsewhere. Many of the young cats there will be picked up by other people who want to give them a nice place to live.

Thus last year, the small tri-coloured Josi went to her new playmate Sara, who lives more than 350 miles away from here.

Little Le Curly has found a wonderful place in Austria with lisping Frankie, who was very sad when his girlfriend Phoebe died a few months ago. Le Curly is now called Sammy. Both immediately became really close friends, and together are quite mischievous during the day.

Jerry, whom I've already written about, has also settled in very quickly with his four new roommates.

I would so much like to meet the cats on the farm. However I would need quite some determination, as walking there takes four days and I can't open the doors at home yet. I also believe that my staff would not like it if I also stank like cowpie.

In any case, the cats there are very well. Thanks to the care packages from our friends, there is plenty of food and the vet regularly looks after them on the farm.

🐾 Nasty coevals

It is 5:30 AM: In the morning this unfriendly character called *'Weekend'* is here again. Of course I have to inform Daddy immediately by pressing my butt into his face and farting.

He apparently is not particularly excited about this *'Weekend'* and is therefore probably quite peeved off. He throws me out of my bouncy castle with a growl and plays possum again.

In my desperation I go to Mommy and bite her several times on her fingers so that my warning is not completely in vain.

She responds immediately and shouts

"Stop it right away!"

Then she says: *"Now you've done it again and ruined the 'Weekend'."* I am therefore in the opinion that my warnings are effective.

That's why I don't really understand why she grabs me and makes the comment, *"this is enough!"* while locking me in the bathroom.

Boring! It is so incredibly boring when you are locked up in a bathroom with no one to play with. I first meow very softly and later properly that I am dissatisfied with the current overall situation.

After I still notice no response beyond the bathroom door, I sit and claw at the door as a sign of life. Apparently somehow my staff already knew that I would do this, because the door is made of a material that you can't carve tattoos or autographs on.

Because I meowed for about two hours without success and scratched on the bathroom door, I was so tired that I occupied the basket from Aunt Molly and fell asleep from sheer boredom.

Aunt Molly is allowed to remain in the bedroom because she does not yet notice the *'Weekend'* intruder and is dreaming in her chair about Caruso.

I'm pretty sure that I owe all the trouble in the early morning to just this horrible *'Weekend'*.

Next time when *'he is'* at the door again, I will just be up earlier to warn my staff more intensively, not to even let him in.

He only creates trouble!

🐾 Kitchen mathematics,

At lunchtime Mommy is in the kitchen and prepares food for herself and Daddy. She has been looking forward to, as she said, *"a thousand little helpers"* to come around and that *"you cannot even peel potatoes without anyone sneaking around between the feet."*

I guess that I should teach Mommy some arithmetics, because we're only four cats in the household and not a thousand. Her attempt to distract us with fresh bowls full of cat food is then only partially successful. Because I eat my ration the fastest of all and then immediately am able to help her with the cooking again. I just do not know why she aligns just because I misinterpret the whole potato skins as pretty patterns on the kitchen floor.

Boiled potatoes are now one of my new favourite foods, which cannot be said of raspberry yogurt.

My aunts like candy but I prefer something hearty such as pasta or boiled potatoes. Let's see what's on my staff's menu tomorrow. I have decided to regularly do more tasting.

Actually by the way, dumplings are so delicious and I cannot get enough of them, as you can see.

🐾 Everything 'different'

Today, everything is pretty weird. Daddy and Mommy constantly look at me, shake their heads and say, *"Something is not right here."*

They discuss that three veterinarians, two veterinary nurses and a farmer cannot all be so incredibly wrong. They mention that *"something is missing"* and they want finally have certainty and this concerns me.

How now? Do I look different from my aunts and other cats?
Apparently, because Daddy looks at me and says while checking,

"I'm not a vet, but there actually is something missing, this can't be true."

So, when I look at me like that, I cannot determine with the best intentions, that something is missing. I have two ears, two eyes, a nose, a mouth and four paws and see no problem with my overall appearance.

A short time later my staff puts me in the shipping box and again in the direction of the veterinarian. Do they want to prick such sharp needles into my back again or clean my ears with the gruesome cotton swabs?

Nothing at all, the vet is greeting me with the words:
"Ah, there is our little Willy again and his eyes have meanwhile healed excellently."

Daddy and Mommy excitedly talk with her and I think it is certainly about me. But now I'm also really curious as to what it is all about.
The vet takes me up and turns me on my back, which I do not like. Then she grabs me between the hind legs and pushes them apart. Wait a minute!

And then there's a sentence I will never forget in my entire life:

"We were all completely wrong, it's a girl!"

What? A girl? Me? Now my world collapses or should I be happy? Questions and more questions have occurred to me and I cannot find any answers.

Daddy and Mommy comment with laughter:

"This little bitch was just kidding with us,"

and the vet also laughed heftily with them.

My staff has to decide whether they should continue to call me Willy or not. Daddy thinks my name should in future be Milly, because only the 'W' has to be turned upside down and it also sounds good.

Mommy says that she might call me Wilhelmine in the future. Please no! I'd prefer that she will continue to call me Willy. I would like it much better than a conservative name for me, just as any woman would to avoid everything that makes her seem old.

Fortunately, I don't have to fear that I'm going to be cast out of my new home because Daddy said that it doesn't matter now whether three or four girls live in the house and if he needs a male cat, he can pat Caruso. In addition, the staff finally needs a reliable cat as a tripping hazard, toe biter, food taster, treats thief, bed squatter, aunt frightener, keyboard trampler and when it comes to the expulsion of the *'Weekend'*.

I don't think it's so bad that I'm a girl. Whether I'll sometimes also be like Aunt Salsa?

When I look at people, the girls always have advantages:
You get invited more often, and can, in contrast to men, wear skirts, paint the fingernails and you may get a wolf whistle on the street.

I am now waiting for whoever will give me a wolf whistle.

🐾 Beyond the horizon

For a long time now, I've been observing my aunts walking through the doors almost daily. These doors are always closed to me. Through one door I can see a bit of what lies behind it. Not much, because in front of it is a wall, but left and right of it there is plenty of room with a bunch of green stuff; people call it a meadow.

I've also often sat on a couple of open windows in the house, but my staff have put grid everywhere in front of them and you feel like you  are in prison. Supposedly the fly screens should prevent flies, but I've discovered that you can use these things as a step ladder which is ideal if you want to know the height of the window.

Whenever I sit there, I hear interesting sounds and occasionally smell the scents of other animals and people when they come over. This is similar to the large square box in the living room, which my staff calls tube or television. It doesn't even have a scent and anyhow, they usually fall asleep in front of it, because the people in the box are either so boring or so stupid.

Whenever I walk behind my three aunts and also want to exit the door, the way is blocked by my staff. I was out there very briefly a few weeks ago, but in this perhaps thirty seconds, I did not really notice how it is out there. But today everything is different. They go with me to the door and open it, without standing in my way.

"Today is the day that you may go outside for the first time. We'll accompany you on your way there, show you everything and then you can explore the area for yourself."

Oh, that's exciting! Somehow I'm afraid to go out, but I'm too curious about this world out there and what to expect.

I'm sure I'll meet my aunts and many other cats who will accompany me on my way and I carefully put one foot over the threshold. I breathe the air around me, listen to the sounds and walk down the four steps of the staircase.

My gaze wanders and I am overwhelmed by all these impressions. I think I will still experience many adventures, because:

The day is still long …

Here my diary comes to a preliminary end and I completely forgot to introduce you to my own staff.

This is Daddy and me.

I owe him so much that I am still alive, thank you very much! I wanted to spend the rest of my life with him but Mommy was packing me and my mate Salvatore in a basket and went far far away to a place somewhere in France because she believes everything is better there. I even couldn't say good bye to Daddy and probably I will never see him again.

Lastly, I greet all my friends, even from the Internet. Thanks and with your persuasion, Daddy could dictate my diary, because I simply don't hammer out the letters with ten fingers properly.

Unfortunately I can't dictate Daddy a continuation of my diary.

It's a pity …

Meet Willy at facebook:

www.facebook.com/willyfanclub

or watch all of his Videos on YouTube:

www.youtube.com/user/Errol01